READ TOGETHER
WITH COZY & CUDDLE

CUDDLE'S CONCERT

Written by Elizabeth Taylor
Illustrated by Colin Petty

Colour Library Books

Cuddle loved singing in his bath.

"Bubbly, bubbly, bubbly, having a bath is so lovely.
I scrub from my toes to the tip of my nose
And my fur feels so shiny and fluffy!"

Cuddle loved singing in his bath. "What a great song!" he laughed to himself. He sang another song even louder than ever.

"Let's have a concert," he said.

"I could be a famous singer!" cried Cuddle, jumping up and sending bubbles everywhere. "The crowds would cheer and clap and shout 'More! More!'" He bowed deeply to a pretend audience. Then he had a brilliant idea.

"Let's have a concert in Woolly Wood," he said. In an instant he was out of the bath and drying himself.

He made a poster about the concert.

Cuddle set to work at once. "There should be lots of different acts to make it a really good show," he thought to himself. So he made a big poster and pinned it to a tree where everybody would be sure to see it.

"What's this?" asked Mr. Mole, who was passing by. He read what the poster said.

Local acts
wanted for
Cuddle's Concert
The singing star
of Woolly Wood
Apply to Cuddle

"I'm going to sing," he told Mr. Mole.

Local acts wanted for Cuddle's Concert
The singing Star of Woolly Wood. Apply to Cuddle.

"I'm going to sing," Cuddle told Mr. Mole. "I'm the singing
Star of Woolly Wood! What can you do?" But before Mr. Mole
could answer, Cuddle burst into song.

"What do you think?" asked Cuddle when he had finished singing.

"Uh huh," coughed Mr. Mole, not sure what to say. Cuddle didn't sound like a singing star at all. He sounded terrible. But Mr. Mole was very polite. "I . . . er . . . I can juggle," said Mr. Mole, tossing some stones into the air and catching them.

"Great!" said Cuddle. "You can be a star, too!"

"I can juggle," said Mr. Mole.

"We can dance!" said the baby rabbits.

Then Cuddle hurried around to Mrs. Rabbit's house to tell her about the concert. "I'm going to sing," he said, "and Mr. Mole is going to juggle. What can you do?"

"We can dance!" said the baby rabbits, and they showed Cuddle how well they could dance.

"Very good," said Cuddle. "Listen to this!" And he began to sing.

"What a noise!" thought Mrs. Rabbit.

"I can roller-skate," said Blossom.

Then Blossom came whizzing by on roller-skates.

"Hi, Cuddle!" she called, doing a triple spin and coming to a halt. "What's this I hear about a concert? Can I be in it?"

"Yes," said Cuddle. "But what can you do?"

"I can roller-skate, of course," laughed Blossom.

"I'm going to sing," said Cuddle. And he started singing again.

Blossom did not think Cuddle was a very good singer but she didn't want to upset him, so she just said, "Got to hurry!" and skated off very quickly.

Cuddle was very excited. He rushed home and wrote lots of invitations for the concert. "This concert is going to be the best ever," he thought. "I must ask Cozy Bear to play the piano for us. He's sure to help."

Cuddle wrote lots of invitations.

Soon the whole village was looking forward to the concert. But Mr. Mole, Mrs. Rabbit and Blossom were worried.

"Everyone will laugh when Cuddle sings," Blossom told Cozy Bear. "He'll be terribly upset. He thinks he's a wonderful singer!"

"Everyone will laugh when Cuddle sings," said Blossom.

"He can't be *that* bad," said Cozy Bear, laughing.

"He is," said Mr. Mole. "His singing is terrible!"

"I'm sure you're all making a fuss about nothing," said Cozy Bear. "But I'll see what I can do."

"His singing is terrible!" said Mr. Mole.

It wasn't long before Cuddle arrived. "I thought perhaps you'd help me practice my singing," he said, holding out the music.

Cozy Bear sat at the piano and began to play. Cuddle took a deep breath, and started to sing.

"Oh dear!" groaned Cozy to himself. "What a noise!"

Cozy thought of a plan. The others were right. Cuddle must not sing at the concert.

Cozy thought of a plan.

He hid the music in the biscuit tin.

The next day, before Cuddle came to practice, Cozy hid the music in the biscuit tin. Now Cuddle couldn't sing!

"I'm so busy," Cuddle told him, flopping into a chair. "I've sorted out the lights, made curtains for the stage, and found costumes for everybody. There's so much to do!"

"Maybe you shouldn't sing as well," suggested Cozy Bear.

"But I'd hate to disappoint everybody," said Cuddle. "I want to practice. Where's the music?"

"Oh dear," said Cozy Bear, pretending to look for it. "I can't find it anywhere. Er . . . let's have something to eat instead."

"Good idea," agreed Cuddle. "Got any biscuits?"

But Cuddle wanted a biscuit.

He opened the tin and found the music.

Before Cozy Bear could stop him, Cuddle had opened the biscuit tin — and found the music!

"How did it get in here?" Cuddle asked in surprise.

Luckily he didn't wait for an answer. He dragged Cozy Bear over to the piano and began to sing.

It was the night of the concert.

"I'm sorry," Cozy Bear told the others. "I did my best but I couldn't stop Cuddle from singing."

At last it was the night of the concert.

Cuddle opened the curtains and bowed deeply to the audience. "Before Mr. Mole does his wonderful juggling, I'd like to sing."

Mr. Mole juggled four balls in the air.

"Quick, Mr. Mole!" whispered Cozy Bear, and he pushed Mr. Mole onto the stage before Cuddle could start.

Mr. Mole began to juggle four coloured balls in the air. The audience clapped with delight — and Cuddle had to slip off the stage without singing a note!

When Mr. Mole finished, Cuddle was busy helping Mrs. Rabbit to tie all the baby rabbits' dancing shoes. He was so busy he forgot to sing. Then he helped Blossom fix a wheel on one of her roller-skates.

Cuddle was so busy, he forgot to sing.

The show came to an end. Everybody cheered.

All evening Cuddle was busy. He didn't have a moment to himself. When the show came to an end, he was worn out!

All the performers danced back on stage for the final bow. "Three cheers for Cuddle!" called someone from the audience. Everybody cheered. "Hurrah! Hurrah! Hurrah!"

"What a success!" thought Cuddle happily as he climbed into a hot bath that night. Then he remembered — he hadn't sung once at the concert! "Never mind," he said. "I can always sing at the next concert!" He picked up the soap and started to sing his favourite song. "Bubbly, bubbly, bubbly . . ."

"I'll sing at the next concert," Cuddle said happily.